Cynthia Rylant • Arthur Howard

MOTOR MOUSE
& VALENTINO

Beach Lane Books   New York   London   Toronto   Sydney   New Delhi

BEACH LANE BOOKS
An imprint of Simon & Schuster Children's Publishing Division
1230 Avenue of the Americas, New York, New York 10020
Text © 2021 by Cynthia Rylant
Illustration © 2021 by Arthur Howard
Book design by Irene Metaxatos © 2021 by Simon & Schuster, Inc.
All rights reserved, including the right of reproduction in whole or in part in any form.
BEACH LANE BOOKS and colophon are trademarks of Simon & Schuster, Inc.
For information about special discounts for bulk purchases, please contact Simon & Schuster
Special Sales at 1-866-506-1949 or business@simonandschuster.com.
The Simon & Schuster Speakers Bureau can bring authors to your live event. For more information
or to book an event, contact the Simon & Schuster Speakers Bureau at 1-866-248-3049 or visit our website at
www.simonspeakers.com.
The text for this book was set in Raleigh.
The illustrations for this book were rendered in mixed media.
Manufactured in China
0721 SCP
First Edition
2 4 6 8 10 9 7 5 3 1
Library of Congress Cataloging-in-Publication Data
Names: Rylant, Cynthia, author. | Howard, Arthur, illustrator.
Title: Motor Mouse & Valentino / Cynthia Rylant ; illustrated by Arthur Howard.
Description: First edition. | New York : Beach Lane Books, [2021] | Series: Motor Mouse books | Audience: Ages
0-8. | Audience: Grades 2-3. | Summary: Motor Mouse takes a hot air balloon ride with his brother Valentino and
neighbor Horatio, decides to teach Valentino to drive a car, and spends a day with Valentino at the Funfair.
Identifiers: LCCN 2020055380 (print) | LCCN 2020055381 (ebook) | ISBN 9781534492950 (hardcover) |
ISBN 9781534492967 (ebook)
Subjects: CYAC: Mice—Fiction. | Brothers—Fiction.
Classification: LCC PZ7.R982 Mor 2021 (print) | LCC PZ7.R982 (ebook) | DDC [E]—dc23
LC record available at https://lccn.loc.gov/2020055380
LC ebook record available at https://lccn.loc.gov/2020055381

For my brother, Michael
—A. H.

CONTENTS

THE FLIGHT OF UNCERTAINTY

Motor Mouse was a very good driver, and this was a good thing since his deliveries took him all over town. There was this box to Stafford Road, that box to Hudson Street, the other box to Bishop's Circus. He always had things well in hand when it came to driving.

But flying: Motor Mouse had never flown in anything before.
He enjoyed being close to home, wheels on the ground.

And when he had a day off, he mostly liked a good read.

So when his neighbor Horatio invited him on a hot-air balloon ride with the balloon club, Motor Mouse was very uncertain.

"I have never flown before," said Motor Mouse.
"Oh, it's fun," said Horatio. "Quite a view."
"And the landing?" asked Motor Mouse.
"Barely a bump," said Horatio.

Motor Mouse was still uncertain.

"May I bring my brother?" asked Motor Mouse.

Whenever his brother, Valentino, was along, Motor Mouse felt more adventurous.

"Certainly!" said Horatio. "We ballooners welcome everybody!"

And that is how Motor Mouse and his brother, Valentino, found themselves at sunset in a wicker basket attached to a giant hot-air balloon.

Valentino was much more keen on taking the ride than was Motor Mouse. He brought many flight perks: binoculars, maps, and so forth.

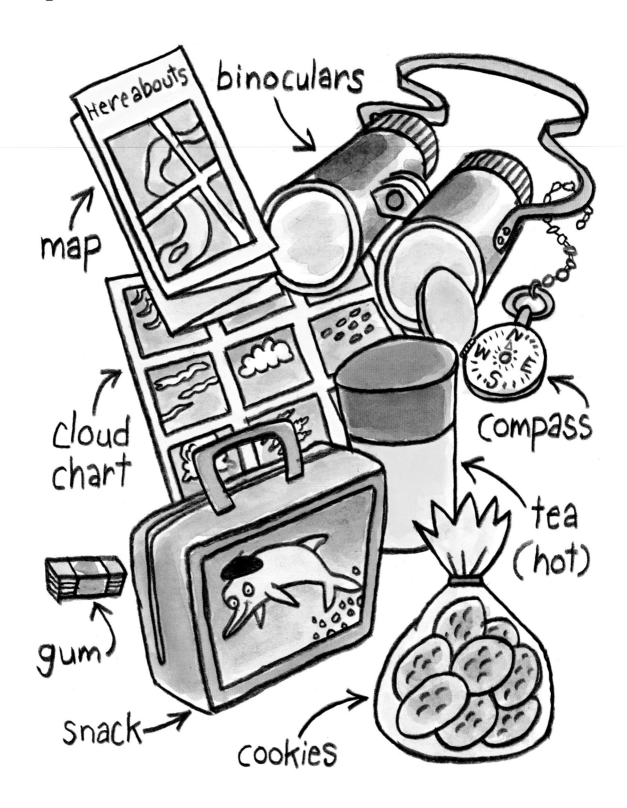

juice →

Motor Mouse just brought a bottle of juice.

The ground crew got the balloon
fired up and they were off.

It was amazing!
The sky is so quiet, thought Motor Mouse.

That is, it was, until a couple of birds
stopped by to talk about the weather.

But after they left: quiet. The land below: beautiful.
It was a short ride, as Horatio had to get home early
for his mother's birthday.

They landed in a hayfield with barely a bump.

And when they got out of the basket, Motor Mouse
borrowed Valentino's binoculars to look back up at the sky.

A Scooter
OF ONE'S OWN

One day Motor Mouse said to Valentino, "I think it is time you learned to drive a motorcar."

"Why?" asked Valentino. "I have a scooter."
Valentino loved his scooter. He had even given it a name: Freddy.

"If you learn to drive a motorcar, we could take a long trip," said Motor Mouse. "We could take turns driving. We could have the world on a string."

Valentino frowned.

"I think that motorcar company has sent you another brochure," he said.

"Even so," said Motor Mouse, "wouldn't you like a motorcar of your own? Something with a roof?"

"I have a hat," said Valentino.

"Let's just give it a go," said Motor Mouse.

So Valentino got behind the wheel of Motor Mouse's motorcar. He started it up.

"Now just press the gas pedal and go," said Motor Mouse.

Valentino pressed the gas pedal. He did not just go. He *zoomed.*

"Brake! Brake!" shouted Motor Mouse.

Valentino stopped the motorcar.
"I miss Freddy," he said.

Motor Mouse sighed.

"I don't understand what is so special about a scooter," he said.

Valentino brightened.

"I'll show you!" he said.

They went into the garage, and Valentino
rolled out his scooter.

"First," said Valentino,
"it is a very nice shade
of green."
　　Motor Mouse grunted.

"Second," said Valentino,
"it has handlebars."
　　Motor Mouse sniffed.

"And third," said Valentino, "it's my best friend.
Besides you."

Of course! Motor Mouse finally understood because
his motorcar was his best friend. Besides Valentino.

Then Valentino gave Motor Mouse
a ride about town on his scooter.
    And it was grand!

ASSORTED AMUSEMENTS AND PRIZES

The Funfair was in town, and Motor Mouse was excited.

He loved funfairs almost as much as he loved his motorcar, and that was a love as big as the moon.

Motor Mouse and his brother, Valentino, made a plan to go to the Funfair first thing Saturday morning.

"Don't oversleep," Motor Mouse told Valentino.

Motor Mouse never overslept. He had deliveries to make Monday through Thursday, so he was on his toes the moment the sun came up.

"I never oversleep," said Valentino.

"You have been oversleeping all your life," said Motor Mouse.

"Only slightly," said Valentino. "And only when I'm dreaming a dream."

"And when you eat too much pudding the night before," said Motor Mouse.

"It depends on which flavor," said Valentino.

"No pudding and no dreams," said Motor Mouse.

"I'll be up with the sun," said Valentino.
"I love the Funfair!"

On Saturday, Motor Mouse and Valentino were first in line when the Funfair opened.

The Ferris wheel was already spinning, the jugglers were juggling, and the barkers were calling, "Have a go!"

Motor Mouse and Valentino looked at each other. Have a
go they would!

They tried their hand at Ding-the-Bell. They threw darts at boards and balls at baskets.

But still no prizes!

"I think the World's Greatest Candy Floss will improve our aim," said Motor Mouse.

"I couldn't agree more," said Valentino.

After eating their candy floss, Motor Mouse and Valentino were too full for games. They chose the Haunted House ride instead.

They took their seats.

"Don't squeak," said Motor Mouse.

"I'll try," said Valentino.

The Haunted House ride was dark and creepy, and sometimes a creature popped out of a closet. Every time, someone squeaked.

"I knew you would," said Motor Mouse when the ride was over.

"Yes," said Valentino. "Let's go again!"

Motor Mouse and Valentino stayed at the Funfair a long time, even after dark. Riding the Ferris wheel was best after dark.

Then before they went home, they tried Ding-the-Bell one more time.

And they both won a prize! It was a marvelous end
to a marvelous day.
Indeed, life was full.